The Wedding Present

by

Adèle Geras

Illustrated by Joanna Carey

First published in 2Q01 in Great Britain by
Barrington Stoke Ltd, Sandeman House, Trunk's Close,
55 High St, Edinburgh EH1 1SR
www.barringtonstoke.co.uk

This edition published 2005

ISBN 1-842993-48-8

Printed in Great Britain by Bell & Bain Ltd

A Note from the Author

A few years ago, I bought six plates from a pottery. These make me happy every time I look at them because of their wonderful colours. I began to think about the rest of my crockery. Every single cup and saucer, plate and mug mentioned in this story is real and may be found in my cupboards.

The people in the story are entirely invented and so is what happens to them.

Some people are very sniffy about love stories, so I wanted to write one that wasn't sentimental at all. I hope I've got it right.

20648

Contents

Chapter 1
Thursday, August 24, 8:00 p.m.

Jane felt terrible. She sat on the train staring out of the window and listened to the sound of the wheels on the track. I'm glad I can't see what I look like, Jane thought. I bet I look as awful as I feel. Rain streamed down the glass in thin lines. Terrible weather, to go with my terrible mood, she thought. It's not like summer at all.

Jane had made lists all her life. One list was of 'Things To Do'. She made a new one every day. Another list was called 'Shopping'. There was a list of 'Books To Read'. There was another of 'Films To See'. But the most important list of all was the 'Long-Term Aims List'. This said things like:

1) Have my own pottery exhibition
2) Visit Nepal
3) Have a baby

Fat chance of a baby now, she thought and was surprised to find there were tears in her eyes. She blinked them away.

There was another item to add to the Long-Term Aims List now:

4) Find a bloke. A decent bloke. Not one like Matt.

Matt was history. She had thrown him out of her flat about three hours ago. He would not be coming back. She could do without him. Quite apart from anything else, he was married. This last fight was probably all for the best.

At least, I don't have to feel guilty any more, she thought. I don't have to think about *Her*. Jane did not like to give Matt's wife her proper name. It made everything much worse somehow.

How come you fell for that bastard with his baby blue eyes? Jane asked herself. Didn't you see that the relationship was going nowhere? He was never going to leave his wife. Jane knew that. Matt had made no secret of it.

Everything was OK at the beginning. Jane had no ideas about marriage in her head at all. She left that sort of thing to Rosie, her older sister.

"Rosie's married," she had told Matt one day. "She's the most married person I know. Happy with her home. She's got a lovely daughter, Ellie. She enjoys her job too. But I'm not like her. I want to do something special with my life."

And look at you now, Jane said to

herself. Have you done anything with your life? Have you heck! No. You've wasted two years on a good-looking swine who wouldn't even give you a lift up north when you needed one.

Jane felt her cheeks turning red with anger. Here she was lugging a large cardboard box packed with six plates, six cups and saucers and six soup bowls all the way up to Manchester on the train. Her suitcase was too small to take the box and she couldn't carry both. So she'd had to get a railway trolley at the station. It was a drag messing about with it and getting the whole lot on to the train and on to the luggage shelf.

Jane had always prided herself on

travelling light. Now here she was feeling like one of those people who couldn't go anywhere without taking all their belongings with them. Bloody Matt! Jane felt like kicking him.

She tried not to think about what would happen to her and the box when they reached Manchester Piccadilly station. She would sort that out later.

"Excuse me," said a voice. Jane looked up, startled. The young man in the seat opposite her was speaking. He was speaking to her. Damn cheek!

Before she could think of what to say, he went on, "I'm sorry, only you looked so miserable, I thought a coffee might cheer you up. I'm off to the Buffet. I can get you one if you like."

"Thank you," Jane said. Suddenly, a coffee sounded like what she most wanted in the whole world. She looked at the man. He was tall and very thin. He wore round, metal-rimmed glasses like John Lennon's and he had brown hair that fell forward over his face. He did not look like an axe murderer.

Jane said, "White. No sugar. Thanks."

When the young man came back, Jane thanked him again.

"That's OK," he said. "I don't make a habit of speaking to people on trains, only ..."

"I can see why you thought I was looking miserable," said Jane. "But I'm more annoyed with myself than miserable, if you want to know. I've just dumped my lover. I used to call him my boyfriend, but that makes him sound like a kid, doesn't it? He's over 30. He might gloat at my misery and I refuse to give him that satisfaction."

The young man took a sip of his coffee. Jane went on, "Good riddance, really. He was married. I should never have taken up with him in the first place. He never cared about me. Take today. I really needed a lift in his car. I've got a heavy box of crockery and it's hard carting it about on a train. I just saw red when he said he couldn't take me to Manchester. It was the last straw. So it's goodbye, creep!"

8

"Crockery ... why are you carrying crockery around, if you don't mind my asking?"

"It's a wedding present. My niece is getting married in Manchester. I'm giving her some crockery. I'm a potter. I make plates and things."

"Cool," said the young man. "I'm getting off at Manchester too. I can help you with the box if you like. I've only got my rucksack."

"You're very kind," Jane said. "What do I owe you for the coffee, by the way?"

"Forget it," he said with a smile. "You look happier already."

The train slowed down as it came into the station. Jane put her suitcase by the door and waited with her new friend till everyone else had got off. Then they picked up the cardboard box together and carried it off the train. They were right beside a trolley park.

"My lucky day," Jane said. Her friend put the box and her suitcase on the trolley and Jane started to wheel it towards the exit.

"Right, then," he said. "Lovely to chat to you. I hope you have a good wedding. Bye."

"Bye," Jane called, "and thanks for everything."

He smiled and waved and strode away.

I never asked him what his name was, Jane thought. I'm a bloody fool. He was nice. It's not often you meet a really nice person. I should have found out what he was called, at least. And why didn't he ask me what my name was? He didn't fancy me, that's why. He was just being kind.

Jane sighed and pushed the trolley to where her brother-in-law, David, always parked his car.

Chapter 2
Friday, August 25, 10:00 a.m.

Jane's sister, Rosie, was frowning. She was concentrating on decorating the wedding cake.

"I don't know why you're doing that yourself," Jane said.

"What do you mean?" asked Rosie.

The cake was set out on the kitchen table. Rosie was piping pink sugar flowers on to the smooth, white icing.

"Most people," Jane said, "pay someone else to do the food for a wedding."

"I'm a good cook," Rosie said. "You're always telling people that. You say, 'My sister is a good cook. You should see what she can do'. Well, Ellie's my only daughter. I hope she'll only ever get married once. I'd like to make a special and lovely day for her. It's fun getting everything ready, isn't it? Aren't you enjoying yourself?"

"Of course I am," Jane said. And if she didn't think about her own troubles, it was true. She loved visiting her sister. Rosie was ten years older than Jane. Her house was beautiful. Her husband, David, spent all his spare time in the garden. For weeks he had been getting the flowerbeds ready for Ellie's big day. Tomorrow, she was going to be married in the garden. The grass was so smooth that it looked like green velvet. The tables and chairs were all ready on the patio. The sun was going to shine. It always did for Rosie. Rain would not dare to fall on Ellie's wedding day.

Jane envied her sister and loved her at the same time. She wished her nothing but good things. She didn't mind that Rosie's life was perfect.

My life isn't perfect, Jane thought. I'm the scatty sister. My life is always a mess. It's Rosie who has a tidy one.

Their mother had died of cancer just after Jane was born. The girls' grandmother came to live with the family. Their father was useless. He was lovable but useless. He adored his daughters, but he was no good round the house. He was the kind of man who really and truly couldn't boil an egg. He lived for his students and his books.

So Granny looked after the house and Rosie looked after Jane. She was the one Jane looked up to and obeyed. If Granny or Dad wanted Jane to do something, they asked Rosie to tell her. Jane always did what her older sister said.

Jane hated school. Rosie loved it and was good at everything. Jane left as soon as she could and went to Art School.

Rosie went to college and then became a teacher. She married when she was twenty. Now she taught Food Technology in the sort of school that was every parent's first choice.

Her husband, David, went to Medical School and became a doctor. Over the years they had saved money. They had paid off the mortgage on their house. They lived a comfortable life.

Rosie was as good a cook as Delia Smith. She even looked a little like Delia, but with dark red hair. Everyone always felt at home in Rosie and David's house.

"Your kitchen," Jane said, "looks like the set for a TV programme. It's the dresser. I've always wanted one. I could display my pottery on the shelves."

"Get one, then," said Rosie. "There's no reason why you can't. There's room in your kitchen."

"I know there is, but you have to have the right kind of lifestyle to go with a dresser. Do you know what I mean? A husband. A child. A proper job. A kitchen you aren't ashamed of. You know what a mess mine is."

"Your kitchen is artistic. It has pictures leaning against the wall and a bowl of fruit you're busy painting that is still drying at the other end of the table. Also, you have paint in pots where jam ought to be."

"Right. And now that I've started on the pottery, there's another kind of mess taking over as well."

Rosie stood back to look at the cake. "There," she said. "What do you think?"

"It's beautiful," Jane said. And it was. The pink sugar blobs really did look like tiny roses.

Ellie came into the kitchen. She went up to the cardboard box that Jane had put beside the door last night.

"What's this, Jane?" Ellie was forbidden to use the word 'Auntie'. Jane said it made her feel too old.

"Never you mind," Jane said.

"It's my wedding present, isn't it? Go on, tell me. It is, isn't it?"

Jane smiled. "Well, of course it is."

"Can I open it now? It's quite big! I wonder what it is?"

"Honestly, Ellie, you may be nearly twenty, but you're just as bad as you ever were. You must wait till Dan's there to open it. It's for both of you. You're just like your Mum. She could never wait, either. Christmas was awful. She used to feel the parcels under the tree. Then she lay awake, trying to guess what was in them. And Granny always told a story about when Rosie was young and ..."

"... she opened her presents in the middle of the night. Then she sellotaped them up again. You've told me that story before!" Ellie sighed. "I'm off. Stuff to do."

Jane made a face. "Help, am I as boring as all that?"

Rosie laughed, "No, she's going to spend the next hour or so on the phone with Dan. Young love. They can't wait to be married."

"Dad and Granny never found out, did they? About the parcels. But you told me. You always told me all your secrets. You still do."

Rosie sat down. She stared at the three layers of cake. For a long while, she didn't say a word.

"Rosie, what's wrong?" Jane was suddenly worried.

"I don't," she said and hesitated, "I don't tell you everything. But I will. I've been wanting to. I just couldn't find the words. Not on the phone. I wanted to tell you to your face."

Jane could feel her heart pounding. "Tell me what?"

Rosie pushed her hair back with one hand. She gave Jane an agonized look. "Tell you about Joe."

"Who's Joe?" Jane asked. As she spoke, David came in through the back door. His arms were full of cut flowers.

"I could murder a cup of coffee," he said. He glanced at the finished cake. "That really is a work of art."

Jane and Rosie exchanged a glance. All talk of Joe would have to wait for another time. Whoever Joe was. How amazing, Jane thought, Rosie having a secret!

"We'll take the cake into the dining room," Rosie said. "Then I'll put the kettle on."

Her voice was almost normal. Only Jane noticed the wobble in it. David didn't. He put the flowers into a bucket near the sink. Rosie and Jane moved the cake off the kitchen table.

"I'll have my coffee in my gardener's mug," David called out.

The gardener's mug was huge. It was handpainted with flowers. It was the only one left of a set of six. The others had all been broken.

When the coffee had been handed round Jane whispered, "Are you OK? When can we talk?"

"I'm fine," she whispered back. "He'll go out again in a minute. It'll wait."

Jane sipped her coffee. The morning sunshine made bright stripes on the kitchen floor. What was Rosie going to tell her? And who was Joe?

Chapter 3
Friday, August 25, 1:30 p.m.

Rosie and Jane were stacking the dishwasher.

"David and Ellie think they're on to a good thing," she said. "They couldn't escape quickly enough. Doing the dishes is usually their job."

They had eaten lunch off David and Rosie's honeymoon plates, which were brightly painted with olives and vine leaves. They had gone to Portugal and found these plates in a market. Rosie had wrapped them in her clothes and they had brought them back in the boot of their 2CV nearly 22 years ago.

"And you haven't broken a single one?" Jane said.

"The pattern's faded a bit," Rosie said. "But I look after them carefully. They stand for ..." she stopped.

"What do they stand for?" Jane asked.

"You'll think I'm stupid," Rosie said. "But I feel that as long as these plates are

OK, then my marriage is OK."

"There's nothing wrong with your marriage, is there? Don't scare me, Rosie. Your marriage is the one, safe thing in my life."

Rosie said nothing. She looked down at the plate in her hands and put it back on the dresser. Jane said, "Go on, tell me. Is this anything to do with Joe?"

"No, no, of course not," Rosie said. "My marriage is fine. Honestly. I just ..."

"Just what?"

"Went mad. For a bit."

"Tell me about it," Jane said. "Who is Joe?"

"He was a teacher at my school. He's left now. I had a thing with him. For a while."

"An affair. Is that what you mean?"

"I hate that word, but I suppose so. Yes, I had an affair." She made a face. She looked more like Delia Smith than ever.

"Tell me about it. I'll make us some tea."

"I don't know why I spoke about it today," Rosie said. "It's over now. Only sometimes all this gets to me." She waved her hand around the kitchen. "A perfect life can be boring. Joe was ten years younger than me. I used you as an alibi, an excuse for being away. I used to tell David, 'Jane needs me. She's having one of her crises'. Then Joe and I would meet in a hotel for the night. It didn't happen often. I was always scared. I thought I would die if David ever found out."

"Did you love him?" Jane asked.

Rosie shook her head. "Not really. But it was exciting. I wish I could explain how it was. My love for David is like the kind of nice, warm fire you sit by in winter. A cosy log fire. Joe was like a firework. Scarlet. Dazzling. Surprising. But fireworks burn out quickly, don't they?"

"Yes," Jane said. "And fireworks leave those horrid, burnt, black sticks behind."

"That's what I feel like sometimes," Rosie said. "I wanted to end it. I told myself each time we met that this was the last time. Then he left me. A couple of weeks ago. Can you imagine? I should have been relieved. But I was sad. My pride was hurt. He went back to his girlfriend. She wasn't much older than Ellie. He's found a new job in London. So at least I won't have to face him in the staffroom next term."

"Why didn't you tell me before?"

"I was ashamed of myself. You've always thought I was the good one."

Then Ellie came into the kitchen. "You two do nothing but natter. Mum, Dan says can he invite an extra man to the wedding? An old friend's just turned up out of nowhere. Well, he's flown in from the States, actually, where he had a job till last week … and he's the brother of Dan's best man, Greg."

"Stop, Ellie," said Rosie. She had her hands over her ears. "I don't need to know every detail. Of course Greg's brother can come. We can squeeze him in somehow."

"Tell me about Greg," said Jane.

"He's Dan's best friend from university," Ellie said. "That's why he chose him to be his best man. Jane, can Mum spare you for a bit? I want you to come and see my wedding dress. And then I'll show you all my presents. Dad has put them all on display."

"That's just what they do at royal weddings," Jane said, smiling.

"Sometimes," Rosie said, "I wish you and Dan had eloped. It would have saved a lot of trouble."

"You don't mean it, Mum," Ellie said. Then she turned to me. "Come on, Jane. I want your advice about which earrings to wear."

Chapter 4
Friday, August 25, 3:00 p.m.

Jane lost her heart to Ellie when she was a fat, happy baby. Now she was a slim, happy, young woman and Jane still adored her. Ellie's wedding dress hung in a cotton bag on the back of her bedroom door. It was cream silk with a low, square neck and a long veil like a waterfall of lace. For her hair, she had chosen a simple hairband of white roses. The florist would deliver it first thing tomorrow, before the hairdresser arrived.

Jane looked up at the shelf. "You've still got the zebra mug," she said. "The one I made you for your ninth birthday."

"I love it," said Ellie. "Zebras on the outside and sunny yellow on the inside. It makes me feel good."

Ellie lay on her bed, with her back against the headboard. She looked about twelve years old. Jane could hardly believe she was getting married tomorrow. She said, "Well, that's why I gave it to you. It made me happy too."

"Do you still have those Chinese bowls?"

36

Ellie asked. "The ones that belonged to your Granny?"

Jane nodded. There was a painted blue dragon at the bottom of each one. They were soup bowls, but Ellie would eat everything out of them. She would push the food about with her spoon, wanting to see the blue dragons.

Jane said, "When you were a baby, you asked, 'How many spoons till we see the dragon?' And then we would count. 'One, two, three'. Then you shouted, 'More, more!'. You liked covering the dragons up again, too."

"Have you still got them?" Ellie asked.

"Oh, yes," said Jane. "A couple of them

are a bit cracked. I use those for paperclips and drawing pins."

Ellie grinned and changed the subject. "If we unwrap your present," she said, "it can go on display with the others."

"Not yet," Jane said.

Ellie leaned forward. She said, "Can I ask you something?"

"Of course," Jane answered. "Anything."

"Have you ever wanted to get married?"

Jane said, "I'm too selfish. I want to use all my time to paint. And make pottery."

"But what about children?" Ellie asked. "Don't you want children?"

"I've got you," Jane said lightly. "And I've blown it for the moment. Did your Mum tell you I'd given Matt the push?"

"I'm glad," Ellie said. "I've always felt a bit funny about you going out with someone who was married. Now maybe you can meet someone proper. Someone single."

"They're not exactly all over the place, these unmarried men."

"Maybe you'll meet someone tomorrow. There are lots and lots of men coming to the wedding ..."

"Most of them are your age, Ellie. I'm not looking for a toy boy," Jane said, half laughing.

"You never know who'll turn up," said Ellie. "I can't think of anyone at the moment, but there must be someone just right out there."

"One day my prince will come ... is that what you're saying?" Jane laughed.

"Well, why not? Everyone else has got a prince, so why not you?"

"They might look like princes, Ellie, but a hell of a lot of them are nothing but frogs." Jane stood up. "I'm going downstairs now," she said. "I should help your Mum with the food. She's making potato salad."

Ellie pulled a face. "Rather you than me," she said.

Chapter 5
Friday, 25 August, 5:00 p.m.

When Jane got downstairs there wasn't much left to do. Rosie had steamed the new potatoes. She had chopped the chives. The home-made mayonnaise was ready. Everything could be put together and the potato salad would be done.

"*Your* potato salad is the best," Jane said. "There's a secret ingredient that you put in it that you don't want anyone to see. Not even your sister."

"Don't be silly! It's just an ordinary potato salad."

"That's where you're wrong. No-one makes it quite like you do. And in any case, making it for 30 people must be really hard."

Rosie said, "It's no different. It's just bigger. But I don't want to talk about cooking. Tell me what happened between you and Matt. Is it really over?"

Jane thought for a moment before she answered, "Yes. It *is* over. I was dazzled by

Matt. I enjoyed the money he spent on me. He told me I was on the wild side. He thought I was scatty and a bit mad, I think. I was flattered that someone so rich and successful even looked at me."

"What nonsense! What do you mean?" said Rosie. "You may be a bit different from most people in some ways. But you're really special. You're lovely."

Jane laughed. "You think so because you're my sister."

"No," Rosie said. "You're a very rare person. You're gifted. You're an artist."

"Thank you," Jane said. "I think men don't like that. They see that my pottery, or my painting is the most important thing in my life and they feel jealous. I know Matt did. He felt like breaking these plates I'd made for Ellie. I could see how he looked at them. I was spending all my spare time on them. Well, I have all the time in the world for work now, haven't I?"

"That can change at any time," Rosie said. "But don't rush things. Now my ... affair ... with Joe is over, I can see how awful it was. I wake up some nights trembling. My whole life, everything I love, was like a plate wobbling towards the edge of a dresser shelf. Ready to fall and break apart. If David had found out, the whole of my marriage would have been smashed to pieces. I can't believe how lucky I've been. I won't do that again. It just isn't worth it."

"Matt always said his feelings for his wife were quite different from his feelings for me," Jane said. "And I believed him because I wanted to. I was a fool."

"No, you weren't," said Rosie. She transferred the potato salad from the giant mixing bowl to two huge china dishes. "Sometimes we can't help ourselves. You're supposed to get more sensible as you get older, but you don't. Not really."

Ellie came into the kitchen. "Jane," she said, "Daddy says he's moved your box into the dining room and can we *please* unpack it now. Otherwise we won't be able to display your present. We can't wait for Dan."

"Oh, OK," said Jane. "Why not? Are you finished here, Rosie? I want you to see everything too."

"I'm coming," Rosie said. "Just let me put these in the fridge."

Chapter 6
Friday, August 25, 7:00 p.m.

Rosie stared at the crockery laid out on the table. David had put all her dishes out on a long, dark table and the colours glowed in the summer evening light. They were blue like the heart of the ocean; pink like the inside of a rosebud; pale green and white and lemon. The colours swirled together like colours on the inside of a

glass marble. Jane had not meant to paint any objects, but one streak of paint looked just like a feather, one could have been a star and maybe there were flowers in the curve of that cup.

Jane looked around at the others. "Aren't you going to say something?"

"This ... all of this is so beautiful that I just can't think what to say." Rosie was still gazing at the pottery. "You're an artist. You truly are. It's absolutely ... fantastic. I'm amazed."

Ellie kept picking up one plate after another and stroking it. She said, "Mum's right, Jane. How did you do it? These are the most beautiful plates and cups and bowls I've ever seen."

"I don't really know," Jane said. "It's always a bit of an experiment. I never know what will happen when I fire them in the kiln. This time I put a whole lot of coloured glazes on the clay with these thick brushes and this is what they came out like."

"I love them!" Ellie cried and flung her arms round Jane's neck. "And I love you, too. Thank you!"

"It's my pleasure," said Jane. "I hope you both eat from them for years and years."

Ellie's eyes widened. "And if we break one?"

"Don't worry," said Jane. "It's only crockery, after all. I can always make you some more. I don't want you to worry about using them."

"Right," said Ellie. "I was going to keep them for best. Now I'm going to use them every single day and for every single meal."

Everyone laughed. Rosie said, "Well, we're not using them for supper tonight. Come on, Ellie. You can help lay the table."

****

After supper, Rosie and Jane sat on the patio as dusk fell. It was David and Ellie's turn to clear up the kitchen.

"Ellie is so traditional," Rosie said. "Has she told you all about her 'something old, something new' things?"

"Yes," Jane said. "And I'm honoured. Her dress is new of course. And she's borrowing my silver bracelet to wear as something old."

Rosie said, "It feels so strange to think that she'll be leaving home tomorrow for good. Going into her own house. Her own life. It'll be so quiet round here."

Jane looked at her sister. Were those tears, shining in her eyes? She said,

"You've got David. And me. And Ellie too, even if she doesn't live here any longer. Don't you remember the rhyme?

> Your son is your son
> till he gets him a wife,
> your daughter's your daughter
> for all of your life.

Rosie said, "I wish I could make something artistic like you do. Those plates ... do you realize how lucky you are to be able to do that? To make things? To make beautiful things? To be an artist?"

"Of course," said Jane. "But you have gifts too, you know."

"Don't be silly!" Rosie said. "You can't possibly mean teaching Year 7s how to make a decent pizza?"

Jane said, "Cooking is an art. You are someone who makes good food, glorious food every day of your life. And look at that wedding cake. If that isn't art, I don't know what is ..."

Rosie said, "I suppose so. We take the things we can do for granted, don't we? Look at David's garden. It's just beautiful. But if you told him his gardening was an artistic gift, he'd laugh at you."

Rosie stood up. "I'm going to bed now, Jane. It all starts early tomorrow morning with the flowers arriving and the hairdresser coming over to do Ellie's hair. Good night, little sister."

"Good night, Rosie. Sleep well."

Rosie didn't know how lucky she was, Jane thought. She had Ellie. Why was it that people took their children for granted? Just lately, she'd begun to look more closely at other people's children. She'd begun to imagine her own. A few years ago, this would have been out of the question. Now, Jane knew, she wanted her own baby. She'd realized that children were the last thing on Matt's mind. At the time she didn't care. She had been so charmed by Matt that she had lost every bit of sense she ever had. How stupid can I be? And I never thought what his wife might be feeling? She shivered. Never again, that was for sure. She would never look at a married man ever again.

Jane sat on in the velvety August dusk until the first star appeared in the sky. She glanced around to make sure no-one was watching her and smiled. You shouldn't still be so stupid when you're 30. You were meant to be grown-up and sensible.

Then she closed her eyes and made a wish, smiling at what anyone who knew her would say if they could see she was being this soppy.

"Star light, star bright,
first star I see tonight,
I wish I may, I wish I might,
have the wish I wish tonight."

Chapter 7
Saturday, August 26, 10:00 a.m.

"How do I look?" Ellie was smiling. She was standing in her wedding dress at the top of the stairs.

Rosie, David and Jane stood at the bottom of the stairs and watched as Ellie made her way down into the hall. No-one could find any words at first, then Rosie

ran forward and put her arms around her daughter.

"Mind my headband, Mum," Ellie cried.

"I'm sorry, darling. I'm not myself today. I feel quite emotional and silly. I'll pull myself together later, I will, really."

David and Jane both spoke at the same time, "You look wonderful," Jane said.

"Darling, you're beautiful," David said.

And then the guests began to arrive and the house was filled with voices. Rosie guided everyone to the garden, where the sun was shining on the roses.

"Everything's going just as we planned," Rosie whispered to Jane. "All we need now is the groom."

"Is the vicar here yet?" Jane asked.

"Yes, that's him over there, chatting to David. And don't the bridesmaids look sweet?"

The bridesmaids had just arrived in a big, white car. Ellie's two young cousins came rushing into the house. Their mother was calling, "So sorry we're late. Traffic was terrible."

The bridesmaids wore pale blue silk dresses with sashes of darker blue velvet. Their headbands were stitched with tiny, white satin rosebuds.

"Where's Dan?" she said. "He can't be late. What's his best man Greg thinking of?"

"They're probably recovering from the stag night," said David.

As he spoke, the doorbell rang again.

"That'll be them," Rosie said. And it was. Jane opened the door.

"Hello, you two!" she said. "We were worrying about you ..." Her voice faded away as she noticed someone standing behind Dan and Greg.

It was the young man from the train – the one who had been so kind to her. When he saw Jane, he grinned.

"Wow!" he said. "I wished for something and it happened. I can't believe it."

Jane's heart was starting to beat so loudly that she thought someone might hear it. Her wish from last night had also come true.

"Come in, come in," Rosie said and all three men stepped into the house. Dan and Greg were led away by David.

Jane found herself all alone with ... what was his name?

"I don't even know your name. I only know you're Greg's brother," she said, smiling.

"Nick," he said. "I know yours. You're Jane. Dan's told me all about you. When I turned up at Greg's house last night, he was talking about the wedding. At first I thought, well, there must be more than one wedding going on today. But when Dan said Ellie's aunt was a potter and was bringing them a wedding present of crockery she'd made herself, I knew it was you. Right?"

"Right."

"I forgot to ask Dan something rather important," Nick continued. "Perhaps you can help me."

"What?" said Jane.

"Are you married? I mean, you told me you'd chucked your lover, but still, you could have been married. That would have been my bad luck."

Jane laughed. "Why would it have been?"

Nick said, "Truly? You truly don't know?"

Jane shook her head.

Nick sighed. "It's because as soon as I had left the station, I wanted to run back and find you. I thought what a fool I was. Why hadn't I asked your name or where you were staying? I hadn't even got your phone number. Why hadn't I asked you out for dinner while I had the chance? Or if not dinner, then at least a drink or another cup of coffee ..."

Jane was laughing. "Whatever are you talking about? You don't even know me. You're moving rather fast, aren't you? I can't believe this is really happening. I might not be the sort of person you get on with at all."

"I can find out, can't I? So far, from what I've seen, you're great."

Jane said, "Have you wondered at all what I might think about you?"

Nick said, "I just took it for granted that you'd like me. I'm smashing, really! Try me and see."

Jane shook her head. "You're mad! Or else you've been at the champagne. Can we take it slowly, please?"

"If I must," Nick said. "But can we make a start right away? Will you sit next to me at this wedding?"

"I think that can be arranged," said Jane.

"Now why don't you show me the garden?" Nick said. He held out his arm. Jane took it and together they stepped out into the sunshine.

****

The wedding was over and Ellie and Dan had driven off to the airport in the white wedding car. Rosie and David were having a quiet drink on the patio with a few old friends. Jane had taken Nick to see the crockery she had given Ellie and Dan.

He looked at each piece in turn. He picked up every one and turned it carefully in his hands, before putting it down again.

"They are beautiful." Then he looked at Jane. "So are you."

Suddenly, his arms were around her. He tilted her chin up and kissed her gently on the mouth. He said, "Will you make some more plates like this for us?"

Jane was going to say something sensible like, isn't it a bit soon to be planning a life together? But the words seemed to melt away before she could say them. Later. They would talk seriously later.

For now, she closed her eyes and gave herself up to something that felt real and wonderful. Something that might even turn out to be love.

Barrington Stoke would like to thank all its readers for commenting on the manuscript before publication and in particular:

Tilly Brignall
Carola Conlan
Laura Green
Caroline Holden
Kelly Jones
Rosie Jones
Isabelle Kaufeler
Steven Lee
Zoe Lyon
Victoria Nowak
Dorothy Porter
Lorraine Sloggett
Moira Thomson
Shona Thomson

Become a Consultant!

Would you like to give us feedback on our titles before they are published? Contact us at the email address below – we'd love to hear from you!

E-mail: info@barringtonstoke.co.uk
Website: www.barringtonstoke.co.uk

More great books from Barrington Stoke!

No Stone Unturned
by Brian Keaney

Lisa Foster likes to go walking on the lonely Cornish cliffs. It's one place she can get away from her violent husband. That's where she meets Simon, a rich, successful author. He talks her into leaving David. But Lisa's husband is the kind of man who will stop at nothing to keep his hold on her – in life or in death.

The day she walks out on her husband starts a series of tragic and horrific events that will haunt the village of Brede forever.

You can order *No Stone Unturned* directly from our website: www.barringtonstoke.co.uk

More great books from Barrington Stoke!

Stalker
by Anthony Masters

An unseen presence creeping up behind you. Threats of violence behind closed doors. Sarah inhabits an uncertain world where it seems no-one can be trusted – least of all the people who say they care. Running away is not the answer. It only leads to fresh terror with no clear means of escape.

Is the final outcome a happy one? You decide.

More great books from Barrington Stoke!

Prisoner in Alcatraz
by Theresa Breslin

No-one gets out of Alcatraz. And now, by a terrible twist of fate, Marty has ended up there. Inside the harshest prison in America. Marty's there for life. Or is he? Some of his fellow inmates have an escape plan. Will it work? Can they manage to break out of Alcatraz?

You can order *Prisoner in Alcatraz* directly from our website: www.barringtonstoke.co.uk